CHEEPY CHICK'S HOLIDAY

BY LUCY KINCAID

ILLUSTRATED BY PAMELA STOREY

BRIMAX BOOKS · NEWMARKET · ENGLAND

Cheepy Chick has a shop. The shop is full of jars. The jars are full of sweets. There are yellow ones, brown ones, white ones, pink ones and green ones. Cheepy Chick sells a lot of sweets. Cheepy Chick is always busy.

Rob Rabbit wants brown sweets. They are on the top shelf.

Cheepy Chick gets the ladder. Up she goes. She gets the jar. She brings it down.

Cheepy Chick puts some brown sweets in a bag.

Rob Rabbit pays for the sweets.

"Thank you," says Rob Rabbit.

Cheepy Chick puts the jar back on the shelf. She comes down the ladder. Molly Mouse comes into the shop. Molly Mouse wants to buy pink sweets. They are on the middle shelf.
Cheepy Chick moves the ladder along.

Cheepy Chick goes up the ladder. She gets the jar from the shelf.

"I do not want pink sweets now," says Molly Mouse. "I want white ones."

The white sweets are on the next shelf. Cheepy Chick comes down the ladder. She moves the ladder along. She goes up the ladder.

Polly Pig comes to the shop. Little Hamster and Bob Hedgehog come with her. Cheepy Chick is asleep.

"Wake up," says Polly Pig.

"Are you ill?" says Little Hamster.

"I have been very busy," says Cheepy Chick. "I am so tired."

"You need a holiday," says Polly Pig.

"Who will look after the shop?" says Cheepy Chick.
"I will look after the shop," says Polly Pig.
"I will help Polly," says Little Hamster.
"So will I," says Bob Hedgehog.
"Go and get ready," says Polly Pig.
Cheepy Chick gets ready to go. Cheepy Chick is happy.

Cheepy Chick packs her bag. She puts in her hat. She puts in her scarf. She puts in her coat. She is ready to go.

Polly Pig stands at the door. She waves goodbye. Little Hamster waves goodbye. Bob Hedgehog waves goodbye.

They all say, "Have a good time."

Cheepy Chick is on a train.
It goes a long way. Cheepy
Chick sits by the window.
She looks out of the
window. She can see
snow. It looks cold. Cheepy
Chick likes the snow.
"I will be there soon," says
Cheepy Chick. Cheepy
Chick is happy.

Cheepy Chick has lots of
fun. She likes the snow.
The snow is cold. Cheepy
Chick is not cold.
Her hat keeps her warm.
Her scarf keeps her warm.
Her coat keeps her warm.
Cheepy Chick falls over.
The snow is soft. She is
not hurt. It is fun.

Pat Penguin helps Cheepy Chick. He shows her what to do. Cheepy Chick goes very fast. She can stop when she wants to. She does not fall over.

"I like going fast," says Cheepy Chick.

"I like being on holiday," says Cheepy Chick.

Cheepy Chick sends a card to the shop. Little Hamster reads it. It says, "Wish you were here."

"So do I," says Polly Pig.

"So do I," says Little Hamster.

"So do I," says Bob Hedgehog.

Cheepy Chick is home again. Polly Pig is glad to see her. Little Hamster is glad to see her. Bob Hedgehog is glad to see her.

"We have been so busy," they say.

"We feel tired now," they say.

Cheepy Chick does not feel tired. She does not need the ladder. She hops up to the jars of sweets.

"My holiday did me good," says Cheepy Chick.

"We can see that," says Polly Pig.

They are all happy.

Say these words again

sweets	snow
full	cold
goodbye	busy
middle	thank you
holiday	tired
waves	happy
window	ready